FRANKLIN PARK PUBLIC LIBRARY

FRANKLIN PARK, ILL.

Each borrower is held responsible for all library material drawn on his card and for fines accruing on the same. No material will be issued until such fine has been paid.

All injuries to library material beyond reasonable wear and all losses shall be made good to the satisfaction of the Librarian.

Replacement costs will be billed after 42 days overdue.

Helen Keller

A Level Two Reader

By Cynthia Klingel and Robert B. Noyed

The Child's World®

Helen Keller could not see, speak, or hear. Even so, she became a very famous person.

Helen Keller at the age of about twenty-two

Helen was born in Alabama on June 27, 1880. When she was just one year old, she became very ill.

The house where Helen was born →

Helen got better. But she could no longer see or hear. She did not learn to speak as a young child.

The next few years were very hard for Helen and her family. Helen could not tell people what she needed.

Helen sitting for a photograph →

Helen's parents found a teacher to help her. The teacher's name was Annie Sullivan. Annie came to live with Helen and her family.

Annie used touch to teach Helen. She spelled words onto Helen's hands. The first word Helen learned was "water."

The water pump where Helen learned her first word →

Helen was a smart girl. She learned very fast. People everywhere wanted to know about this amazing girl.

Helen gave speeches and wrote books about her life. She needed Annie to help her because she still could not see or hear.

Helen Keller at her desk →

Helen and Annie were together until Annie died. Then, a woman named Polly Thomson helped Helen with her speeches.

Helen died on June 1, 1968. She was 87 years old. No one will forget the work of this brave woman.

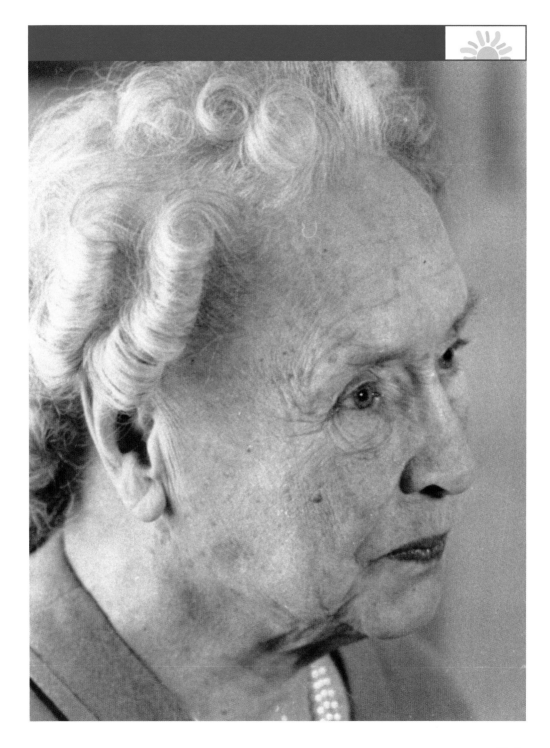

Index

To Find Out More

Books

Graff, Stewart and Polly Anne. *Helen Keller: Crusader for the Blind and Deaf.* New York: Bantam Doubleday Dell, 1991.

Hurwitz, Johanna. *Helen Keller: Courage in the Dark.* New York: Random House, 1997.

Lundell, Margo. *A Girl Named Helen Keller.* New York: Scholastic, 1995.

Web Sites

Helen Keller International
http://www.hki.org
To read about Helen Keller's life and this organization's work to prevent blindness.

Note to Parents and Educators

Welcome to The Wonders of Reading™! These books provide text at three different levels for beginning readers to practice and strengthen their reading skills. In addition, the use of nonfiction text gives readers the valuable opportunity to *read to learn*, not just to learn to read.

These leveled readers allow children to choose books at their level of reading confidence and performance. Level One books offer beginning readers simple language, word choice, and sentence structure as well as a word list. Level Two books feature slightly more difficult vocabulary, longer sentences, and longer total text. In the back of each Level Two book are an index and a list of books and Web sites for finding out more information. Level Three books continue to extend word choice and length of text. In the back of each Level Three book are a glossary, an index, and a list of books and Web sites for further research.

State and national standards in reading and language arts emphasize using nonfiction at all levels of reading development. The Wonders of Reading™ books fill the historical void in nonfiction for primary grade readers with the additional benefit of a leveled text.

About the Authors

Cynthia Klingel has worked as a high school English teacher and an elementary teacher. She is currently the curriculum director for a Minnesota school district. Writing children's books is another way for her to continue her passion for sharing the written word with children. Cynthia is a frequent visitor to the children's section of bookstores and enjoys spending time with her many friends, family, and two daughters.

Robert Noyed started his career as a newspaper reporter. Since then, he has worked in communications and public relations for more than fourteen years for a Minnesota school district. He enjoys writing books for children and finds that it brings a different feeling of challenge and accomplishment from other writing projects. He is an avid reader who also enjoys music, theater, traveling, and spending time with his wife, son, and daughter.

Published by The Child's World®, Inc.
PO Box 326
Chanhassen, MN 55317-0326
800-599-READ
www.childsworld.com

Photo Credits
© AP/Wide World Photos: 5, 10, 13, 14, 17, 18, 21
© Bettmann/Corbis: 2, 6
© Stock Montage, Inc.: cover, 9

Project Coordination: Editorial Directions, Inc.
Photo Research: Alice K. Flanagan

Library of Congress Cataloging-in-Publication Data
Klingel, Cynthia Fitterer.
Helen Keller / by Cynthia Klingel and Robert B. Noyed.
    p. cm.
ISBN 1-56766-952-2 (library bound)
1. Keller, Helen, 1880–1968—Juvenile literature.
2. Blind-deaf women—United States—Biography—Juvenile literature.
[1. Keller, Helen, 1880–1968. 2. Blind. 3. Deaf.
4. Physically handicapped. 5. Women—Biography.]
I. Noyed, Robert B. II. Title.
HV1624.K4 K55 2001
362.4'1'092—dc21

00-013169

24